A Perfect Plan!

Suddenly Emma and Charlie heard a loud sniffling noise. They turned and saw two big tears running down Lindsey's cheeks. Charlie reached over and put her arm around Lindsey's shoulders.

"You've been acting weird lately," Emma pointed out. "What's the matter?"

"Aunt Mariel wants me to come and live with her in Boston," Lindsey blurted out.

"No!" Charlie gasped, shocked.

"Yes, and she's been talking to my father about it. I hear them at night."

"Did you tell your father you wouldn't go?" Emma asked.

Lindsey looked down. "I tried to talk to him a couple of times, but I freeze up. I just can't say anything."

"I sure don't think I'd want to live with your Aunt Mariel," said Emma. "No offense, but she'd drive me crazy."

"I know," Lindsey said. "Do you think *I* want to?"

"She wants some little girl she can turn into a perfect lady," Emma continued. "So if you don't want to go, you're going to have to force yourself to be a real pain in the neck for as long as it takes. I know it's hard because you're a good kid, but you're fighting for your life."

"I guess you're right," said Lindsey.

"Of course I'm right," Emma assured her. "Now, here are some things you can do. . . ."

No Way Ballet

A TWIST OF FATE

by Suzanne Weyn

Illustrated by Joel Iskowitz

Troll Associates

Library of Congress Cataloging-in-Publication Data

Weyn, Suzanne.
   A twist of fate / by Suzanne Weyn; illustrated by Joel Iskowitz.
      p.   cm.—(No way ballet ; #2)
   Summary: When ten-year-old Lindsey worries that she may have to go
to live with an aunt in Boston and leave her widowed father alone,
her friends from school and ballet class support her in various
ways.
   ISBN 0-8167-1621-8 (lib. bdg.)   ISBN 0-8167-1622-6 (pbk.)
   [1. Fathers and daughters—Fiction.   2. Aunts—Fiction.
3. Friendship—Fiction.]   I. Iskowitz, Joel, ill.   II. Title.
III. Series: Weyn, Suzanne. No way ballet ; #2.
PZ7.W539Tw   1990
[Fic]—dc19   89-30585

A TROLL BOOK, published by Troll Associates,
Mahwah, NJ 07430

Printed in the United States of America.

10 9 8 7 6 5 4 3 2 1

One

Lindsey Munson peeked through the blinds of her bedroom window and watched the dented blue hatch-back pull into the driveway. In the dusky light she saw her father get out of the car and walk around to the passenger's side. He opened the door, and out stepped a tall blond woman wearing a long navy-blue coat.

Aunt Mariel.

It was only six o'clock but it was already starting to get dark, making it hard for Lindsey to see her aunt clearly. She watched for another minute as her father took Aunt Mariel's two large suitcases from the back-seat. Then Lindsey stepped away from the window and sat on the edge of her twin bed.

Lindsey remembered very well the last time Aunt Mariel had visited, even though it was over three years ago, when Lindsey was only seven. Lindsey's mother was still alive then, and Lindsey remembered complaining to her mother about Aunt Mariel on almost every day of the visit.

*　　*　　*

"She acts like everything I say is dumb," Lindsey had griped as her mother sat at the kitchen table, peeling potatoes for supper. "And everything she says sounds like a lecture." The scene was still clear in Lindsey's mind. Her mother wore jeans, as usual, and the sleeves of her gray Fordham University sweat shirt were pushed up casually. Her long hair, blond and curly, just like Lindsey's, was pinned up at the sides.

"Mariel's almost forty, and she hasn't been around children in a long time," her mother had explained, handing her a peeler and a potato.

Lindsey remembered how the kitchen had looked then, too. It was never neat as a pin, but her mother kept it orderly and colorful. There were always fresh fruits and vegetables in bowls, and red-checked dish towels were folded through some of the drawer handles. It had been Lindsey's favorite room, the place where she and her mother did most of their talking. Since her mother's death, though, the kitchen had changed. Her father just didn't have the same knack for making it cheerful. In fact, it was pretty messy a lot of the time.

"You and Aunt Mariel are so different," Lindsey had commented as she had struggled with the potato that kept slipping out of her hand and rolling onto the floor. "It must be weird having a sister who's ten years older than you are. Are you sure she really *is* your sister?"

Her mother had laughed as she picked Lindsey's half-peeled potato off the floor and rinsed it under the faucet. "You sound just like your father. He and Mariel don't hit it off too well, either. I know Mariel can be overbearing. Still, she's my sister, so we're stuck with her for just a little while longer. Don't let her bother you. She means well."

*   *   *

When her father had announced last week that Aunt Mariel was coming to visit once again, Lindsey greeted the news with mixed emotions. On the one hand, her memories of Mariel weren't particularly fond ones. Yet Lindsey couldn't help wondering if this time she'd see something of her mother in Aunt Mariel—something she'd forgotten or been too young and childish to notice on her aunt's last visit. And now that she was ten, maybe Aunt Mariel wouldn't treat her like a little kid anymore.

Part of her hoped that either she or Aunt Mariel had changed enough so that they would feel close to one another. It would be like getting a small piece of her mother back.

Lindsey heard the front door close. "Lindsey, we're here," her father called up the stairs.

She stuck her head out of her bedroom doorway. "I'll be right down," she called back.

Lindsey quickly checked her appearance in the full mirror behind her door. She remembered that Aunt Mariel was superneat, so she had stuck her medium-length blond curls behind her ears to make her hair seem more under control. *No good,* she thought. *That makes my ears look humongous.* She fluffed her curls back around her face. Her hair had grown lately; it was almost shoulder length. *Maybe this sweat shirt should go, though,* she told herself as she pulled the bleached-out blue shirt over her head.

Finding something to replace it wasn't that simple, though. Her entire wardrobe consisted mostly of jeans, T-shirts, and sweat shirts. Finally, she remembered the white blouse with the lace collar her father had bought

3

her last Christmas. She pulled it from her bottom drawer. The pins were still in it. When she removed them and shook the shirt out, there were deep creases where it had been folded. "Oh, well," she muttered, "it doesn't look that bad."

She put on the blouse and buttoned it. She was shocked to see how much she'd grown in almost a year. She rolled up the too-short sleeves and pressed the creases down one last time. *Why am I so nervous?* she asked herself. *This is just my aunt, not the Queen of England. I look okay.*

"Come say hello to Aunt Mariel," her father called again.

"I'm coming," Lindsey replied, bounding out of her room and down the stairs. "Hi, Aunt Mariel," she greeted the woman seated on the sofa. Lindsey didn't know if she would have recognized her aunt on the street. She was much heavier than the last time Lindsey had seen her, and her blond hair was now cut very short. She also wore large, wire-frame glasses which she hadn't had before.

"My goodness, slow down on those stairs," Aunt Mariel said. "It sounds like a herd of buffalo are coming down."

"Oh, sorry," Lindsey apologized.

"I can always tell where Lindsey is," said her father, coming in from the kitchen with three colas in his large hands. "She's not exactly the quiet type." He narrowed his eyes in a quizzical expression when he saw Lindsey in her wrinkled white blouse and blue jeans, but he didn't say anything. He just set the glasses on a magazine on the coffee table and took one glass for himself.

Lindsey crinkled up her nose at her father. "I'm not

4

that loud." Her father looked tired and pale, and his green eyes had a flat look. Lindsey figured he was exhausted from driving out to the airport after working all day at the telephone company.

"It always amazes me how much Lindsey looks like Terry," Aunt Mariel said to Lindsey's father, as if Lindsey weren't even there.

"I know," agreed her father, sitting on the edge of the large blue easy chair, jiggling the ice cubes in his glass. "She definitely has Terry's hair and her gray-blue eyes. But I see a lot of myself in Lindsey, too."

"You do?" asked Mariel skeptically. "I suppose Lindsey has your build; square. And she's certainly got your round nose."

Lindsey suddenly felt like a circus clown with a big red, round nose. She touched it quickly. It wasn't *that* round. Lindsey didn't like the way this conversation was going. She looked at Aunt Mariel's large suitcases. She had obviously packed quite a bit of clothing, and Lindsey wondered just how long she was planning to stay.

Just then, the phone in the kitchen rang. "I'll get it," said Lindsey, eager for an excuse to get away from this analysis of her looks.

"Hello," she said as she grabbed the receiver of the wall phone.

"Hi. It's me." Lindsey was glad to hear her friend Charlie Clark on the other end. In the last month, Charlie and Emma Guthrie had become her two closest friends. All three of them were in the same fifth-grade class at Eastbridge Elementary, but that wasn't how they'd come to be friends.

Their friendship began on the day they were forced

6

by their parents to enroll in Miss Claudine's School of Ballet at the Eastbridge Mall. It had been Charlie's mother's "great idea" to enroll Charlie, and she wanted to get other kids from Charlie's class involved so they could form a car pool. Mrs. Clark's idea had hit Lindsey's father at the perfect moment—just when he'd received a note from the principal saying that Lindsey had been fighting with some boys in the schoolyard. Ever since her mother died, her father had worried that Lindsey didn't have enough feminine influences in her life. Ballet, he decided, would be the perfect remedy for Lindsey's tomboy ways.

"Is your aunt there yet?" Charlie asked.

"Yup," Lindsey replied.

"So?"

"So what?"

"So, how does she seem?" Charlie shouted. "You haven't talked about anything all week except your aunt's visit and whether or not you'd be able to stand her this time."

"She just got here. She looks different, kind of older and fatter. So far she seems the same, though . . . sort of . . . bossy."

"Did you find out how long she's staying?"

"I don't know, but she's got these two humongous suitcases." *Humongous* was a word Lindsey had picked up from Charlie. Emma had, too. The three of them liked to use it whenever they could.

"Humongous," Charlie repeated. "That's bad news."

Lindsey looked at the kitchen clock above the sink. "It's past six-thirty. How come you're not watching *Entertainment Wrap-Up?*" she asked. Charlie's great passion in life was TV, and she never missed *Entertainment*

7

Wrap-Up. It was a TV show where a man and woman talked about other TV shows and the stars on them.

Charlie groaned. "My dumb brothers are watching some stupid football game. There's three of them and one of me, so I don't have much choice. Football has got to be one of the jerkiest things on earth."

"Come on," Lindsey argued, "it's neat the way they bash into each other and all."

"No way," Charlie insisted. "It's gross."

Lindsey thought it would be great to have three big brothers to watch TV sports with, but she knew Charlie didn't feel that way. Charlie liked her brothers most of the time, but she hated sports all of the time.

"My mother's calling me for dinner, I've got to go," Charlie said. "Your father's driving to ballet tomorrow, right?"

"Yeah, it's his turn. I'll remind him." The girls said good-bye and hung up. Lindsey could hear her father and aunt talking in the other room. She heard the phrases "since we moved to Boston" and "Miles's business" and knew they were talking about Aunt Mariel's home and her husband Miles. They had stopped picking apart Lindsey's looks. The coast was clear to go back in.

"That was Charlie," Lindsey announced. "Don't forget you have to drive us tomorrow, Dad."

Aunt Mariel went pale. "Don't tell me you let her go out on dates, Frank!" she gasped.

Lindsey and her father looked at one another, confused. Then her father laughed. "No, Charlie is a girl. She's in Lindsey's ballet class."

Suddenly Aunt Mariel was impressed. "How long

8

have you been studying the dance, dear?" she asked, talking directly to Lindsey for the first time.

"I guess about a month," Lindsey answered.

"And how do you find it?"

"It's not hard to find," Lindsey answered, darting a confused look at her father. "It's on the lower level of the mall."

Aunt Mariel coughed. "No, dear, I mean, how do you like it?"

Lindsey had to think about that. She and Charlie were tied for worst dancer in the class—they were just slightly worse than Emma, who was pretty bad. No matter how hard Lindsey tried, she just was *not* graceful. Coordinated, yes. Strong and fast, yes. Graceful, no.

She'd hated, dreaded, *detested* (as Emma liked to say) ballet class at first. But in the course of the last month her feelings had changed a little. She liked their teacher, Miss Claudine, a lot. Although Miss Claudine was very dramatic, with her graceful, flowing dance skirts and long, swirling hair, there was also something very natural and down to earth about her. Miss Claudine loved ballet so much that Lindsey had found herself swept up in the teacher's enthusiasm.

The other reason she liked the class was her friendship with Charlie and Emma. Lindsey had never had many girl friends before. She'd always hung around with boys, playing sports and being "one of the guys." She still liked sports, but she found that having girl friends was nice, too. There were things she could say to Emma and Charlie that she wouldn't have felt comfortable talking about with a boy.

Lindsey finally answered her aunt's question. "I like it okay, I guess."

"Show Aunt Mariel some of the things you've learned," suggested her father.

Lindsey shot him a pained look. "Dad," she whined, "I can't."

"Why not?"

"It's too embarrassing."

"Come, dear, let me see," Aunt Mariel encouraged. "I studied ballet for many, many years. I can tell you if you have it right."

Lindsey started to lift her hand up in front of her to begin an arabesque, then stopped. She felt too foolish. She was self-conscious enough in class. Doing the ballet movements here in her living room in front of her father and someone who was practically a stranger was too much. She just couldn't get herself to do it.

"I don't want to," she insisted, suddenly angry at being put in this awkward spot.

"Frank, do you let her speak to you in that tone?" Aunt Mariel questioned Lindsey's father.

"Lindsey, show Aunt Mariel some ballet, please," her father commanded sternly.

Lindsey just couldn't. "I said I don't want to, okay?" she snapped.

"That's it, Lindsey," said her father, rising to his feet. "I think you'd better go to your room until you can be friendlier."

Lindsey felt her face blaze red with anger and embarrassment. She turned on her heels and stormed up the stairs. Inside her bedroom she sat on the edge of her bed with her arms folded tightly across her chest. Hot tears rolled down her cheeks. How could her father treat her that way—and in front of Aunt Mariel!

Aunt Mariel hadn't changed at all. It had taken her

10

less than an hour to make Lindsey's life miserable. Lindsey heard the sound of raised voices. She cracked her door open to hear what was being said. Her father and Mariel had lowered their voices somewhat.

"I'm sorry for shouting," she heard her father say, "but Lindsey is my daughter, and I'd appreciate it if you'd watch what you say about her."

"Lindsey is also my niece," she heard Aunt Mariel reply. "And for Terry's sake I care about what kind of person she turns into. That's why I'm here."

"She's turning out just fine," her father answered.

"I wouldn't say so from her tone of voice," said Aunt Mariel, "and that awful wrinkled blouse."

The voices faded as her father and Aunt Mariel moved into the kitchen.

Lindsey shut the door quietly. She lay down on the bed and closed her eyes. She suddenly had a terrible knot in the pit of her stomach.

Two

The next morning was Saturday. Lindsey awakened to the smell of bacon frying and pans softly clanging downstairs in the kitchen. She looked at the red numbers on her digital alarm clock. It was only eight o'clock! Sometimes Lindsey and her father had breakfast together on the weekends at the Purity Diner, but her father almost never *made* breakfast. And they never, ever got up before nine on a Saturday. Something strange was going on. Then she remembered Aunt Mariel.

As much as Lindsey wanted to stay in bed, the smell of the bacon was too good to resist. *Well,* she thought, sleepily pulling her blue terry-cloth robe on over her flannel pajamas, *it's nice of her to cook. Maybe she's trying to make up for yesterday.* Encouraged by this thought, Lindsey decided to put the events of last night out of her head and to start fresh with Aunt Mariel this morning.

Lindsey met her father in the hallway. In his half-asleep state, he'd put on his plaid robe inside out. His dark brown hair stood on end at crazy angles. It looked to Lindsey like he'd stuck it in the blender.

He squinted at her with a groggy expression. "Bacon," he managed to say as he yawned.

Lindsey was glad he didn't seem angry with her any longer. Last night he'd brought her supper to her room on a tray and said they'd talk about what had happened in the morning. That was typical of her father's style. He always said he liked to put a little distance between the event and the discussion because he didn't want to talk while he was still angry.

They plodded downstairs toward the kitchen together. "Good morning, sleepyheads," chirped Aunt Mariel. She stood over the stove, nudging a large omelet into shape with a spatula. "There wasn't a thing to eat in that refrigerator, so I picked up a few provisions. Sit! Sit!"

Lindsey and her father looked at one another. The table was set with blue checked napkins that Aunt Mariel must have just bought. There was a glass filled with flowers in the middle of the table next to a pitcher of orange juice and a couple of jars of jam. Coffee was bubbling in the coffee maker. Toast was being kept warm in the toaster oven.

"Mariel, you shouldn't have gone to all this trouble," said Lindsey's father.

"No trouble," replied Aunt Mariel pertly. "Now sit and let me serve this while it's still hot."

The omelet was delicious. Lindsey and her father ate silently. They were not morning talkers, but Aunt Mariel kept up a constant stream of chatter. She talked about how she and her husband Miles loved their new

13

brownstone in Boston, about how sunny and cheerful it was, and how much space they had.

"Thanks for breakfast, Aunt Mariel," said Lindsey. "I'd better start getting ready for . . . class." Lindsey avoided saying the word *ballet* for fear of reminding everyone of the fight last night.

"Me, too," said her father, pushing his chair from the table. "I have to pick up the crew this morning."

"I wish I could drive. I'd do it for you," Aunt Mariel said.

"Thanks, but it's really no problem," answered Lindsey's father just a bit curtly. "I don't mind doing it."

By the time Lindsey showered and put on her jeans, sweat shirt, and sneakers, it was a little after ten, time to leave.

" 'Bye, you two." Aunt Mariel waved from the couch where she was thumbing through a magazine.

" 'Bye." Lindsey waved back as she pulled on her jean jacket and grabbed the red nylon bag which held her ballet leotard, tights, and slippers.

"She sure was cheerful this morning," Lindsey commented in the car as she and her father buckled themselves in.

"She's a regular Mary Sunshine, all right," her father answered sourly.

Lindsey didn't say anything for a few blocks as they drove toward Charlie's house. She sensed that her father didn't feel like talking. Finally, though, she had to ask, "What did Aunt Mariel mean when she said she's here because she cares about me?"

Her father turned to her, surprised. "It's not polite to eavesdrop."

"Sorry. What did she mean?"

14

Her father looked away to his left and then back at her. "She just meant that she wanted to see you. To make sure you were all right."

"Why wouldn't I be all right?"

"Beats me," her father answered. "You *are* all right, aren't you?"

"Yeah, I think so." Lindsey held up her arms and pretended to be checking herself. "I'm okay as far as I can tell."

Her father laughed and reached over to tousle her hair. "You look okay to me, too," he said. "And I'm sorry about last night," he added. "I shouldn't have forced you to show Aunt Mariel your ballet steps. That woman just puts me on edge somehow."

"It's okay," Lindsey answered, relieved that everything was right between them again. "I'm sorry I shouted."

Charlie was already waiting on the stoop of her square brick house, holding her blue canvas ballet bag. When she saw them she stuck her head back into her house to yell good-bye and ran toward the car.

"Hi, Mr. Munson," Charlie said as she climbed into the backseat. She tugged one of Lindsey's curls playfully as a greeting.

Lindsey returned her greeting by turning around in her seat and crossing her eyes at her friend.

"My legs are killing me from those pliés in fifth position that we did on Wednesday," Charlie complained, rubbing her calf through her blue corduroy pants. "Man, they're really murder."

"My legs don't hurt because I hardly bent them," said Lindsey. "How is a person supposed to bend their legs in that position. It's inhuman!"

"What are you talking about?" Mr. Munson asked as he turned the corner toward Emma's house.

"Miss Claudine has us do these weird things that look like slow knee bends at the beginning of each class," Lindsey explained. "They're called pliés."

"Can the other girls do it?" Mr. Munson asked.

Charlie and Lindsey exchanged glances. "Most of them can," Lindsey admitted.

"Then I guess you'll just have to keep at it," said Mr. Munson with a smile.

"We try," Charlie told him with a dramatic sigh, "but Lindsey and I are just hopeless. Emma's hopeless, too—just not as hopeless."

By this time they were pulling into Emma's driveway. Lindsey jumped out of the car and ran up the walkway to the front door. Just as she rang the bell the front door opened.

"Hello, Lindsey," said Emma's petite dark-haired mother. "Emma," she called back into the house. "I said move it!"

Emma came into view wearing a denim miniskirt, yellow knee socks, and black leather tie shoes. She already had on her purple jacket. She'd pulled her long hair into a braid that hung over her right shoulder.

Lindsey was used to the way Emma dressed, but something was different today. Lindsey stared at her friend, trying to figure out what it was.

"Let me see your face, young lady," said Mrs. Guthrie suddenly.

That was it. Lindsey saw that Emma had lined her blue eyes with a deep navy eyeliner. Emma loved to wear makeup, but usually she never put it on until after she left the house.

"Emma, you're not going anywhere looking like that," her mother scolded.

"I don't have time to take it off," said Emma matter-of-factly. "I guess your father will have to leave without me, Lindsey. I'll have to skip class today."

"Oh, no you don't, miss," said her mother. "You can wash it off when you come home. You are *not* going to miss that class."

Emma just shrugged. "Okay, if you insist," she said. " 'Bye." She grabbed her large red-and-black tapestry pocketbook from the front-hall table, and followed Lindsey down the walkway to the car.

"Your poor mother," said Lindsey, shaking her head but smiling at her friend. "I thought you were starting to like ballet class."

"It's okay, but I would never tell my mother that." Emma confided. "It's better if she thinks I still hate it. That way she feels a little guilty and lets me get away with other stuff to make up for forcing me to take ballet lessons. I knew this makeup thing would work. I thought it up last night in bed."

Lindsey looked at Emma with a mixture of puzzlement and admiration. She'd never met anyone like her. Certainly no one else she knew thought the way Emma did. Lindsey and Charlie had discussed Emma and decided she was different from the kids they knew in Eastbridge because she'd lived most of her life in the city—and because her parents were divorced. It seemed to them that either of those things could make a kid grow up a little faster than other kids. The two things together made Emma seem older, and, well, just a little strange. But, Lindsey and Charlie had agreed, that was

17

one of the things that made Emma fun to be with—you never knew what she'd do or say next.

"How's crabby old Aunt Mariel?" Emma asked quietly as they approached the car.

"She was awful last night, but supernice this morning," Lindsey answered. "Maybe she was just tired or something after her trip. Who knows?"

Emma climbed into the backseat next to Charlie while Lindsey returned to her place in the front. Charlie opened her hazel eyes wide when she saw Emma's eye makeup. "Wild!" she whispered.

Mr. Munson headed for the Eastbridge Mall while the girls chattered on about school, the impossible pliés and, one of their favorite topics, the much-detested Danielle Sainte-Marie.

"I get so sick of her bossing me around," complained Emma. "Just because Danielle's a year older and takes intermediate class, you'd think she was supposed to be the teacher instead of Miss Claudine. I wish she didn't have to warm up in our class."

"I can't believe Miss Claudine likes her," said Lindsey. "She's such a snob."

"She just likes her because she has a French name," Emma suggested. "You know Miss Claudine is *bats* over anything that's French."

"I know," muttered Charlie. "She keeps calling me Charlotte, and I have to keep telling her that's not my name."

"But your name *is* Charlotte," said Emma.

"I know, but I wish it wasn't," Charlie replied. "Nobody calls me that. Miss Claudine thinks it's the greatest name because it's French."

"Is Miss Claudine French?" asked Mr. Munson as he entered the mall parking lot.

The girls were silent. "It's hard to tell," Charlie answered at last. "She uses a lot of French words, but she doesn't have a French accent or anything."

Emma shrugged. "Miss Claudine is just Miss Claudine," she said. "She's weird—but nice."

Mr. Munson parked the car near the back door of the mall. Inside the mall, he left them just as they were about to go down to the lower level to Miss Claudine's. "I have to get a few things, so I'll stick around here at the mall," he told them. "See you at one o'clock."

They waved good-bye and headed down to Miss Claudine's. The three girls always felt the same mixture of nervousness, dread, and excitement each time they saw the pink-curtained storefront. Part of each girl wanted to run away just as they'd done at their very first class. But another part had grown to look forward to seeing Miss Claudine and even to learning the new ballet steps.

At the end of every class Miss Claudine told them the story of another ballet. They looked forward to that as much as seeing each other. Miss Claudine's stories were so captivating that the girls felt themselves transported into the magical world of the ballet stories.

But one thing Emma, Charlie, and Lindsey didn't look forward to was seeing bossy Danielle. She was the best dancer in the class, but she certainly wasn't modest about it. Nor could she seem to mind her own business for two minutes. Today she was standing at the doorway when they arrived. Her brown hair was pulled back tightly into the bun she always wore, and her nose and chin were tipped slightly upward in her usual superior expression.

"I hope you girls know you have only ten minutes to dress," she said, looking at her delicate gold watch. "It's ten to eleven."

"Bug off," snapped Emma.

"You're not dressed," Charlie added, looking at the neat blue sweater and blue plaid pleated skirt Danielle was wearing. "What's your excuse?"

"I don't need an excuse," snipped Danielle. "But if you must know, I was busy taking some new students for a tour of the facilities. They're interested in enrolling next session."

"What facilities?" asked Lindsey, gesturing around the front room at Miss Claudine's big desk with the picture of Marion Sweeney—her student who later became a Radio City Music Hall Rockette—hanging on the wall near it. Besides the glass door to Miss Claudine's office and a few straight-backed chairs, there wasn't much to see.

"You wouldn't understand," said Danielle. With that, she turned away haughtily and walked toward the mirrored dance studio.

"That girl really burns me," fumed Emma as they walked into the narrow dressing room.

Danielle was right; most of the other girls were already in their baby blue leotards, pink tights and pink ballet slippers. Charlie, Emma, and Lindsey were soon the last ones left changing.

The girls dressed quickly. Charlie noticed that in the month they'd been taking classes she had gotten over her shyness about dressing in front of the others. Now she just pulled her sweater over her head and scooted out of her pants and into her tights and leotard.

"Hey," said Emma as she smoothed the wrinkles from the ankles of her tights, "isn't that Danielle's dance bag on the bench?"

"Who else would have the initials DS embossed in gold on her bag?" replied Lindsey, pulling on her slippers.

"After I thought of the makeup idea last night I had another little idea," Emma said with a mischievous gleam in her eyes. "Charlie, do you still have that sewing kit in your bag?" Emma asked as she opened Danielle's leather bag.

"Yeah, but you shouldn't go into Danielle's stuff," answered Charlie.

"Don't worry, I'm not going to take anything," said Emma, carefully lifting Danielle's leotard out of the bag. "Give me the sewing kit."

"What are you going to do?" asked Lindsey.

"You'll see," answered Emma mysteriously.

Three

"You girls had better get out to class," said Danielle as she scurried into the dressing room. She quickly pulled her sweater over her head and folded it neatly on the bench. "Get going," she said, noticing that Emma, Lindsey, and Charlie were taking their time.

"It's okay, Danielle," said Emma, twisting her braid. "We'll wait for you."

"That's really not necessary," said Danielle, stepping out of her skirt.

Charlie and Lindsey looked at one another with laughter in their eyes and then quickly went back to straightening their tights.

"And what do you two look so amused about?" snapped Danielle, annoyed.

"Oh, nothing," answered Charlie in a sing-song voice.

"Ooooohh!" screeched Danielle suddenly. She'd slipped both arms into the sleeves of her leotard at once and discovered what Charlie and Lindsey already knew. Emma had sewed the openings of the sleeves shut.

"Ooooohhh!" Danielle screeched again, speechless

with anger. She waved her arms in the air wildly, trying to punch her way through the stitches.

Charlie and Lindsey collapsed onto one another, laughing hysterically. Emma fell back against the wall, laughing in little hiccuping bites of air. She laughed until tears came to her eyes, streaking her navy-blue eyeliner.

"This isn't funny!" screamed Danielle. She tried to wriggle her way out of her sleeves, but found it wasn't so easy to free herself of the leotard. Frustrated and furious, Danielle lunged at Emma and began pounding her with the sewed-up ends of her sleeves. This convulsed Emma with a new fit of laughter as she rolled along the wall, away from Danielle.

"Temper, temper, Danielle," she scolded breathlessly.

"You'd better hurry up, Danielle," said Charlie as she and Lindsey headed out of the dressing room. "You'll be late for class."

Danielle rushed out of the dressing room after them, still waving her closed-off sleeves. "I'm telling Miss Claudine," she shouted.

A group of five girls stood in the front room talking before class. When they heard Danielle shout they turned and looked at her. They quickly noticed her sleeves, and all five began to smile. "Need some help, Danielle?" giggled a thin, blond-haired girl named Tish.

"Yeah, Danielle," said Emma from the doorway to the dance studio, where she stood with Charlie and Lindsey. "It looks like you could use a hand."

Realizing she was making a fool of herself, Danielle turned and stormed back into the dressing room.

"You have great ideas," Charlie said to Emma. "You should write for TV."

"I just couldn't take any more of Miss Know-It-All," said Emma, wiping up her smudged eyeliner with her knuckles.

Just then Miss Claudine stepped out of her office. Her ash-blond hair was pulled back from her face and hung down her back in a long braid. Her sea-green leotard and tights were covered with a knee-length yellow ballet skirt. *"Bonjour, mesdemoiselles,"* she greeted them happily. "Come, let us begin."

She glided past them into the studio. "Today we will have a very exciting class," she said, beckoning them to follow her with a graceful wave of her hand.

Charlie, Emma, and Lindsey lined up with the fifteen other girls at the barre. Miss Claudine turned on the portable record player that she kept in the far corner of the class, and the room was filled with lively—though scratchy—classical music.

The class always began with pliés. All the girls knew the routine. They assumed the first position, with their feet turned out and their heels touching. From this position they bent their knees and slowly descended as low as possible to the floor. Then slowly they rose again.

"Bend deeper, Mademoiselle Lindsey," Miss Claudine coached. "You are a limber young girl, not an old woman."

Lindsey rolled her eyes and tried to get herself to bend her knees farther. Her right knee let out an embarrassing creak. *It's no use,* she thought miserably, *I'm just not flexible.* Lindsey was used to being the best at anything athletic. Until she took ballet she had never realized that it was even possible for her to be bad at

25

something requiring physical activity—but bending just wasn't her strong point.

"Chin up, Mademoiselle Emma. Shoulders down. Smile! No one is torturing you."

Emma raised her chin, lowered her shoulders, and smiled at Miss Claudine for one second. She was starting to enjoy ballet, but she wasn't ready to let anyone know it. She had definite ideas about what was cool to like and what *wasn't* cool to like. Ballet was very uncool in her opinion. She thought it would be much too twerpy to go around saying, "I just love ballet class."

"Has anyone seen Danielle?" asked Miss Claudine, noticing that her star pupil wasn't at her regular spot at the barre. The question caused a round of giggles that left Miss Claudine looking perplexed.

"She's still dressing," Charlie spoke up.

"Hmmm," Miss Claudine mused. "It's not like her to be late. She always helps with this class." Miss Claudine looked to the doorway for any sign of Danielle, and then back to the class. "Now to second position," she instructed.

The girls widened their stance and continued the pliés in second. "Not so wide. Place your feet closer together, Mademoiselle Charlotte," said Miss Claudine.

"Charlie," Charlie corrected Miss Claudine for what seemed to her to be the millionth time.

"Very well, Mademoiselle Clark, feet closer together," Miss Claudine said with a sigh.

Charlie didn't have trouble bending in second position. That was easy. Her problem was staying in time with the rest of the class. When they were up, she was down, and vice versa. She didn't know how she managed to always be doing the opposite of everyone else, but she found it extremely embarrassing.

The class did second-position pliés while Miss Claudine went around the room and checked their placement. They quickly ran through pliés in the third and fourth positions—with the feet turned out but in front of one another. "And now the demi-pliés in fifth," Miss Claudine instructed.

Lindsey groaned as she tried to slide the toe of her right foot so far left that it touched the heel of her left foot. The stretch made the outsides of her thighs burn.

Emma was the most limber of the three girls, but even she still couldn't get her feet to lie flat against each other. The effort made her wobble at the waist. She let out a deep sigh that caused Charlie to turn around and roll her eyes at her friend sympathetically, as if to say, "This is impossible."

"Remember, class," said Miss Claudine, still walking around the room adjusting legs and feet, "you do not bend as deeply in the demi-plié. The main purpose of a plié in this position is to help you take off when you do a jump."

Lindsey tried to picture herself leaping gracefully up into the air, but the picture wouldn't come. All she could see was an image of herself tripping over her own feet and falling on her face.

Miss Claudine watched the class perform their fifth-position pliés for a few more minutes. "Not bad, *c'est bon,* coming along," she said approvingly. Then she clapped her hands for attention and turned the record player off.

"Today we are going to attempt our first jump. It is a small but very pretty jump called an échappé." Miss

27

Claudine demonstrated the jump. She began by assuming the fifth position with her arms gracefully rounded at her sides. She sprang up into the air and straightened her legs out into a wide second position with her toes pointed, and then came down again into fifth position.

She made it look so easy that the class applauded. Miss Claudine smiled. *"Merci,* class. When you master this jump, we'll move on to doing changements de pied. I will show you."

Still in fifth position, she leapt up and quickly switched the position of her front and back feet in mid-air. Then she landed in fifth position again. Once again the class clapped.

Miss Claudine walked to the record player and put on some very sprightly music. "I will show you how these jumps can be combined and repeated for a very nice effect."

She stood in the center of the studio and jumped very quickly, doing a combination of échappés and changements. Charlie shook her head in awe. Miss Claudine made it look like some invisible cord was pulling her effortlessly up into the air and then dropping her gently down. Charlie knew that it wasn't as easy as it looked.

Just then Danielle rushed into the studio looking frazzled and very upset. "I'm so, so sorry to be late, Miss Claudine!" she cried.

Startled, Miss Claudine turned toward Danielle just as she was coming down from a changement. "Oooof!" she groaned as her right ankle turned out underneath her and sent her collapsing to the floor.

"Oh, Miss Claudine! Are you hurt? Are you all right?" the students asked as they crowded around their teacher.

"Fine, girls. I'm fine," said Miss Claudine, rubbing her ankle. But the girls could see she was just being brave. Her pale expression and the tears in her eyes told them how much her ankle hurt. Miss Claudine tried to get up, but she winced in pain and sat back down. "It looks like I need some assistance," she said, smiling weakly at the girls.

Lindsey was the first to shoot out her hand. Miss Claudine grabbed it and pulled herself to her feet. Leaning on Lindsey's shoulder, she moved her injured ankle in a gentle circle. "It's not broken, at any rate," she said.

"Oh, I'm so sorry, Miss Claudine," Danielle wailed. "I didn't mean to startle you, and it really wasn't my fault. These three brats made me late. Do you know what they did?"

Miss Claudine closed her eyes wearily. "Don't worry, Danielle," she said. "I'm sure you had a good reason. But, class, let this be a lesson. Never distract anyone when they are in the middle of a jump. This is exactly what can happen."

Emma smiled. It was just like Miss Claudine to make everything into a lesson—even her own injury.

Miss Claudine tried to put her weight on her right foot and once again winced in pain and leaned back against Lindsey. *Chérie,* help me to that chair if you would be so kind," she asked Lindsey.

Even though she was clearly miserable, Miss Claudine conducted the rest of the class from her straight-backed wooden chair in the corner of the room by the record player.

At twelve-forty-five she clapped her hands to mark the end of class. "I will see you all on Wednesday," she promised.

The class poured through the studio door toward the dressing room. Looking back over her shoulder, Emma saw Miss Claudine hobbling slowly across the room. She was about to offer some help when she saw Danielle dart across the studio and take Miss Claudine's arm.

"I think she's hurt worse than she's admitting," Emma said to Charlie and Lindsey.

They both looked back at their teacher and exchanged worried glances. Miss Claudine was so pale she looked as if she was about to faint.

Four

That Saturday afternoon, Charlie, Lindsey, and Emma sat in Lindsey's living room. Mr. Munson had driven them back from the mall, and then Emma and Charlie had called their mothers to get permission to stay for a while.

"I'm taking a nap," Mr. Munson said with a yawn and went upstairs, leaving them alone to discuss ballet class and Miss Claudine.

"How old do you think Miss Claudine is?" Emma asked as she sat on the floor doodling in the sketchbook she carried in her large pocketbook. Emma's dream was to someday be an artist, and she was always busy drawing something.

"Hard to tell," said Lindsey, sprawled on the couch. "Sometimes she looks like she's in her twenties, but today, when she got hurt, she looked a lot older."

"I hope she's okay," Emma said. "I wonder if she had someone to come and drive her home."

"When you think about it, we hardly know anything about her, really," observed Charlie, who was switching around the TV channels with the remote control. All she could find were sports events, the only shows on TV that held no interest for her. So she watched a couple of commercials before turning the TV off.

"I bet Miss Claudine's life would make a great TV mini-series," said Charlie. "I can see it now, *The Life and Loves of a Ballerina.* The first scene begins in a small but cute street in Paris."

"I don't think she's really French," said Emma, not looking up from her pad.

"It doesn't matter," Charlie told her. "Things are always more interesting on TV than in real life. And it's definitely more interesting to be from Paris than to be from Eastbridge. Anyway, in this Paris street is a little girl dressed in rags. She's poor and dirty, but is she sad? No. She runs up and down the block, spinning and leaping gaily through the air. She's known to all her neighbors as the Dancing Cherry."

"Why do they call her that?" asked Lindsey, flipping over onto her stomach.

"Isn't that what the French always call people, cherry? Miss Claudine called you cherry today."

"That's *chérie,* not cherry," laughed Emma. "It means 'dear.'"

"Oh," said Charlie, blushing. "I always wondered why she was calling people cherries. Okay, so they call her something else, the Dancing . . ."

"The Dancing Rag Doll," offered Lindsey.

"Yeah, that's good," Charlie agreed. "So the Dancing Rag Doll grows up and becomes a beautiful young girl. One day she's dancing past a big mansion, and a very rich, handsome man named . . . Pierre sees her and falls madly in love. And she loves him back."

"But Pierre is engaged to marry someone else, I'll

33

bet," added Emma. "A gorgeous but extremely snobby countess named . . . Danielle."

"Definitely," laughed Lindsey. "What are you drawing, Emma?"

Emma held up her sketchbook. She'd drawn a line down the middle of the page. On one side, she had drawn a picture of Miss Claudine dressed in rags. On the other side was Miss Claudine as the most famous ballerina in France.

"Hey, that really does look like her," said Charlie, taking the sketchbook from her hands.

"I bet that whatever her story is, she's had an interesting life. You can tell just from looking at her," Lindsey said.

"It hasn't been dull, that's for certain," said Aunt Mariel, walking in from the front hallway, wearing neat beige pants and a matching sweater. The three girls stared at her with puzzled expressions. How could she possibly know Miss Claudine's life story?

The truth hit Emma first. Aunt Mariel had only heard Lindsey saying someone's life must be interesting, and she assumed they were talking about *her* life.

"Oh, no, we weren't talking about— " Emma began.

"We were just curious. We didn't want to seem nosy," Lindsey cut Emma off. She realized her aunt's mistake, too, but didn't want her to be embarrassed.

"Not at all," said Aunt Mariel, sitting down in a large, comfortable chair and looking flattered by their interest. "What would you like to know?"

Lindsey looked at her two friends nervously. It was clear that they were going to leave the questions up to her. "I know that you and my mom grew up in New

Jersey until your parents got divorced," Lindsey said. "Then what happened?"

"It was a strange arrangement, I suppose," Aunt Mariel told them. "I stayed with Mom while Terry went off and lived with your grandfather, our father."

"Did that make you sad?" asked Lindsey.

"Terribly sad at first," said Aunt Mariel. "I felt the worst for your mother, being stuck in the little apartment that our father lived in."

"But Mom loved Gramps," Lindsey pointed out.

"Oh, your mother was one of the most loyal people I've ever met. But it couldn't have been easy for her, especially when she came up to Newport in the summer and saw how happy I was with Mom and George."

"Who was George?" asked Emma, who'd been listening intently to Aunt Mariel. Since her own parents had recently divorced, Emma was always interested in stories about families with divorced parents.

"George was my stepfather, the man my mother remarried. He died just three years ago. He was a fine man, a very important man in the financial world, too. He treated me as if I were his own daughter. He made sure I had ballet lessons, piano lessons, and riding lessons. He even bought me a horse of my own."

"Your own horse! Wow!" cried Lindsey, suddenly interested. "Where did you keep it?"

"We had stables on the grounds. George was a fine horseman. Your mother missed out on all those good things—the debutante ball, traveling to Europe, everything." She turned to her niece. "Your mother pretended she didn't care, but I can't believe living alone with our father was easy for her. She had no woman around who could help her through her teen years. That must have been very difficult."

"Mom turned out okay," Lindsey said defensively.

Aunt Mariel glanced quickly around the living room. Suddenly Lindsey saw it through her aunt's eyes. The furniture was a little threadbare in spots. The rug was a little frayed at the corners. Slightly dusty magazines were heaped on the coffee table. Still, thought Lindsey, it looked all right.

"It always amazed me that she *did* turn out to be such a wonderful person," said Aunt Mariel, "but her life could have been so much easier. I always wished I could bring her to live with us in Newport, but your grandfather wouldn't hear of it. I begged and pleaded, but it did no good." Aunt Mariel shook her head sadly at the memory.

"We'd better go," Charlie said, looking at the clock on the shelf over the couch. "My mother said to be standing out front at five. She hates having to get out of the car. Come on, Emma, we'll give you a ride home."

"Walk your friends to the door," Aunt Mariel instructed Lindsey.

Lindsey resisted the urge to tell her aunt that she was going to do that anyway and didn't need to be reminded. She got up and pulled her friends' jackets out of the front-hall closet as they walked to the door.

"It sounds to me like your mother got the better deal," Emma said in a low voice.

"Debutante balls, yuck!" whispered Charlie in agreement.

There was a quick toot of the horn as Mrs. Clark pulled up the driveway. Emma and Charlie ran out the

37

front door, waving to Lindsey over their shoulders. "See you Monday in school," Charlie called.

"Yeah, see you," Lindsey said, waving. She lingered at the door, not wanting to go back and talk to her aunt all by herself.

"Thanks for telling me about your life, Aunt Mariel," Lindsey said briskly when she walked back into the living room. "I'm going to ride my bike around a little before supper, okay?"

"Just a moment, Lindsey," Aunt Mariel said. "I'd like to have a word with you now that we're alone."

"Sure," Lindsey replied, looking at her aunt expectantly.

"Sit," Aunt Mariel said, and smiled warmly.

Lindsey sat down on the couch facing her aunt.

"Did my story about your mother remind you of anyone you know, Lindsey?"

Lindsey thought about it for a moment. "Roger Hudson is a kid in school. His parents are divorced, and he lives with his father, but that's because his mother said she couldn't control him. He's always in trouble and—"

"No, no," Aunt Mariel interrupted. "I was thinking of *you,* dear. You're here living all alone with your father just as your mother lived with her father."

"But my parents didn't get divorced," Lindsey protested.

"No, but I can't help but feel that your life could be easier if you were in a real family, one with a mother *and* a father."

"But my father and me *are* a real family," Lindsey replied, fidgeting on the couch. She didn't like the way this conversation was going. She wanted desperately to run out of the room.

"Your father is a fine man, but it's hard for him," Aunt Mariel said gently. "The phone company just doesn't pay the kind of salary he needs to offer you all the things your mother would have wanted you to have. What I'm trying to say, Lindsey, is that Miles and I would love to have you come and live with us. It would be as if I was finally able to give my sister all the things I wish she'd had."

"But my father . . ." Lindsey gasped.

"Your father and I discussed it last night. He's still only considering it, but if you showed your enthusiasm for the idea, I'm sure he'd come around. Think of how much fun it would be. We have a stable with horses at the summer house in Newport."

"Aunt Mariel, thanks, but . . . I couldn't . . . I . . . Dad," Lindsey stammered.

"It's very sudden, I know," said Aunt Mariel. "You think about it, and I'll continue discussing it with your father. I know I can convince you both that it would be the best for everyone."

Five

It was Emma's mother's turn to drive the girls to Miss Claudine's on Wednesday after school. Lindsey and Charlie always liked it when Mrs. Guthrie drove because she had a tan Jaguar and she drove it quickly, zooming around the turns like a race-car driver.

"Oh, you girls are so lucky," she said with a sigh as she pulled the sporty car up to the back entrance of the mall. "Some of my happiest times were spent in ballet class."

"We've heard, Mom," said Emma dryly as she climbed out of the low front seat. She knew the story by heart. Her mother had dreamed of being a dancer, but she'd had Emma instead.

"I know you secretly love ballet as much as I did, Emma," Mrs. Guthrie said brightly.

"Dream on," Emma replied, twisting her mouth into a disgusted grimace.

Charlie and Lindsey looked at one another. Neither of them could ever believe the things Emma got away with. Both of them knew they'd be in big trouble if they ever used that tone of voice with their parents. Emma's mother just seemed to ignore it—most of the time, anyway.

Mrs. Guthrie walked them down to Miss Claudine's and then left to do some shopping. "I don't see why you can't let your mother know that you like ballet," Charlie said to Emma as they walked into Miss Claudine's front room. "What's the big deal?"

Emma shrugged. "It bugs me that she wants me to love ballet just because she loved it. I'm not her. I'm me."

"I know what you mean," said Lindsey seriously. "My aunt seems to think I'm my mother, and not me."

"It's a drag," Emma sighed. Just then the door of Miss Claudine's office opened and out walked Danielle. She was already dressed for class, and her head was held even higher than usual. She was obviously in a very good mood.

Miss Claudine came out of the office behind Danielle. Emma, Lindsey, and Charlie gasped when they saw her. Miss Claudine was hobbling on crutches! Her right foot was wrapped in an Ace bandage from her toes to above her ankle.

Her long hair was in its usual braid down her back, but instead of her usual leotard, tights, and dance skirt she wore a long-sleeved black corduroy jumpsuit with red buttons down the front. She smiled at her students who gathered around her. "It is badly sprained, I'm afraid, *mes chéries,*" she told them.

"She looks pretty in regular clothes," Charlie whispered to her friends.

"But look how tired she seems," noticed Emma. "Her ankle must really be bothering her." What Emma said was true. The sparkle was missing from Miss Clau-

dine's sharp blue eyes, and she was even paler than usual.

"Don't worry, *mesdemoiselles,*" said Miss Claudine. "We will have class as usual. I will sit and instruct, and Danielle will demonstrate."

The students turned to look at Danielle, who couldn't have appeared happier if she'd won a million dollars. She stepped forward and smiled at the class, nodding her head slightly to them. "Don't worry about a thing, Miss Claudine," she said. "I have everything under control."

"I'm going to gag," said Emma in a loud whisper. Charlie, Lindsey, and the other nearby girls giggled.

Miss Claudine clapped her hands for silence. "I will expect cooperation from all of you, *mesdemoiselles.* I am fortunate to have Danielle, who is able to demonstrate. Now, those of you who are not dressed had better hurry and get ready for class." She sharply clapped her hands twice as a signal for them to get going, and then limped on her crutches back into her office. Charlie, Emma, and Lindsey walked slowly toward the small dressing room.

"Look at her," whispered Charlie, nodding her head toward Danielle, who was now standing at the entrance of the studio and looking in, as if she were overseeing the warm-up. "She's acting like she just won an Academy Award or something."

"She is pretty sickening," Lindsey agreed.

"I don't think I can stand an hour and forty-five minutes of Danielle," said Emma. "How about you guys?"

"I'm with you," said Lindsey.

"Me, too," Charlie agreed.

Without saying another word the three girls quietly

backed toward the front door. They opened it slowly and slipped outside. Then they broke into a run down the wide mall aisle until they were safely away from the pink-curtained storefront of Miss Claudine's.

"Remember, my mother is roaming around here somewhere, so keep your eyes out for her," Emma reminded them.

"I wish that appliance store with all the TVs wasn't so close to Miss Claudine's," complained Charlie. "*Search for Love* is on." *Search* was Charlie's favorite TV show.

"I want to look at earrings," Emma announced. She turned to Lindsey. "What about you?"

"Doesn't matter," Lindsey mumbled.

Charlie and Emma looked at each other, trying to figure out whether they'd try to find a TV screen or a jewelry counter first. Suddenly they heard a loud sniffling noise. They turned and saw two big tears running down Lindsey's cheeks. Charlie reached over and put her arm around Lindsey's shoulders. "Are you all right?" she asked.

"You've been acting kind of weird since Monday," Emma said. "You've been real quiet and all. What's the matter?"

Lindsey stared at the floor. "It's Aunt Mariel," she mumbled, not looking up.

Charlie crooked her mouth and raised her eyebrows at Emma in a helpless expression that asked, "What now?"

Emma shrugged her shoulders. "Maybe we should go sit down somewhere and have some sodas," she suggested.

Charlie nodded and then she and Emma led Lindsey

up the escalator and to a coffee shop in the middle of the mall.

By the time they had settled in and ordered three chocolate milk shakes, Lindsey was over her tears. "So, what's up?" Emma asked kindly.

"Aunt Mariel wants me to come and live with her in Boston," Lindsey blurted out.

"No!" Charlie gasped, shocked.

"Yes, and she's been talking to my father about it. I hear them at night."

"Did you tell your father you wouldn't go?" Emma asked.

Lindsey looked down at her wide, squarish hands spread on the table. "I tried to talk to him a couple of times, but every time I try I freeze up. My mouth goes dry and I just can't say anything."

"But he's your father," said Charlie.

"I know how it is," Emma sympathized. "I used to think I could talk to my parents about everything, but when they got divorced, forget it. They tried to talk to me but I just clammed up. I didn't know what to say."

"Maybe I'm afraid of what he'll say. I don't know," said Lindsey, starting to get misty eyed again. "One day everything is normal. Then this happens."

"I sure don't think I'd want to live with your Aunt Mariel," said Emma. "No offense, but she'd drive me crazy."

"I know," Lindsey said. "Do you think *I* want to?"

A waitress in a blue checked uniform brought their milk shakes. They sipped in silence for almost five minutes before Emma spoke. "Okay, I think I know what you have to do here," she said.

"What?" asked Lindsey eagerly.

"You have to act totally horrible," Emma told Lindsey seriously. "You have to make her believe that you're the most hideous brat who ever walked the face of the earth."

"What good will that do?" asked Charlie.

"Don't you see?" Emma replied. "Her aunt isn't going to want to deal with a horrendous kid. She wants some little girl she can turn into a perfect lady."

"Oh, no! Do you think she plans to send me to one of those debutante things?" groaned Lindsey.

"Maybe," Emma told her. "That's too horrible to even think about. That's why you have to listen to me. This is serious."

"If I act too bratty I'll get in trouble, though," Lindsey protested.

"Look, do you want to end up in a finishing school?" Emma asked impatiently.

"No."

"Then you're going to have to force yourself to be a real pain in the neck for as long as it takes. I know it'll be hard because you're a good kid, but you're fighting for your life."

"I guess you're right," said Lindsey.

"Of course I'm right," Emma assured her. "Now, here are some things you can do. . . ."

Six

Mrs. Guthrie pulled into Lindsey's driveway at a little after six that evening. After class the girls had waited for her in front of Miss Claudine's as if they'd been inside all the time.

"Remember what I told you to do," Emma said, as Lindsey climbed out of the backseat of the Jaguar.

Lindsey sighed. "I'll try."

"Good luck," said Charlie, waving good-bye.

Lindsey just nodded and smiled weakly. The thought of deliberately getting into trouble made her stomach hurt. It wasn't that Lindsey never got into trouble, but when she did it was usually by accident.

Lindsey trudged up the cement path to her front door. She didn't know how to *try* to be bad. She didn't like fighting. She wanted everyone to be happy and to get along. That was just how she was.

Still, Emma's plan did make sense. If Aunt Mariel decided Lindsey was a hopeless brat, she'd never want to take her home to Boston to live. Lindsey would just have to make it up to her father by being extra good after Aunt Mariel left.

She opened the front door with her key. "I'm home," she called.

Aunt Mariel stepped out of the kitchen. She wore a ruffled blue flower-print apron over her gray pants and sweater. Her expression was extremely serious. "I just received a most disturbing phone call," she said.

From the way Aunt Mariel's steely blue eyes bore into hers, Lindsey just knew that the phone call concerned her somehow. She stopped between the front hall and the stairs and waited for her aunt to continue.

"Yes, a Mademoiselle Danielle called from your ballet school. She said you and your two little friends departed from your ballet class before it had even begun. She just wanted someone to know what was going on."

Lindsey's eyes narrowed angrily. "Why, that little creep, Danielle! She's just a kid, like me. She doesn't work for Miss Claudine or anything."

"Did you or did you not attend ballet class today, Lindsey?" Aunt Mariel asked sternly.

"It was a dumb class. Miss Claudine hurt herself, and we would have had to watch that stupid Danielle. We wouldn't have learned anything anyway and—"

"That isn't the point, Lindsey," Aunt Mariel interrupted in a tone that said that she was gravely disappointed in her niece. "You have defied your father's wishes."

"I didn't think of it that way, Aunt Mariel."

"It isn't up to me to decide how to deal with this," Aunt Mariel said, turning back to the kitchen. "Your father had to go to the office for a few hours. I will discuss it with him when he returns."

"Do you have to tell him?" Lindsey asked.

"I most certainly do," Aunt Mariel replied, shocked.

"I think you had better go to your room until he arrives."

Lindsey went upstairs sullenly. She stood at the head of the stairs and listened. Once again she heard the unfamiliar sound of pots clanking and knew Aunt Mariel had returned to whatever she was preparing for supper.

She walked down the short hallway to her father's bedroom and sat on his bed. She picked up the telephone by his bedside and dialed Charlie's number.

Mrs. Clark answered. "No, Charlie cannot come to the phone. She's being punished," Mrs. Clark told her when she asked to speak to Charlie. "Honestly, I don't know what gets into you girls."

"Ummm . . . well . . . thanks, 'bye," said Lindsey, not knowing what else to say. Obviously Danielle had reached Mrs. Clark.

She dialed Emma's number next. "Hi," Emma said when she heard Lindsey's voice. "Did dip-head Danielle call your house?"

"She got Aunt Mariel," Lindsey replied.

"Will she tell your father?"

"Yup," Lindsey said glumly.

"Hmmm," Emma mused thoughtfully. "This is working out great!"

"What are you talking about? My father's going to be really mad at me," Lindsey whispered loudly.

"Exactly, dummy! This works right into our plan. You *want* to get in trouble, remember? Now you have to act like you're not even sorry. Do you think you can do that?"

"Well," Lindsey considered. "I don't think what we did was so terrible, but I suppose we really shouldn't have."

49

"You're hopeless!" Emma shouted. "With that attitude you'll be apologizing in no time. You have to make matters worse by insisting that you had every right to do what you did. Don't back down."

"I don't know, Emma."

"I guess you might as well start packing to go to Boston, then," said Emma coolly, "because that's what's going to happen if you let this great chance to be a brat slip away."

"Okay, okay, you're right. I'll try," Lindsey agreed. "Are you in trouble with your mother?"

"Not yet," Emma answered, her voice dropping to a whisper. "That idiot Danielle left a message on our answering machine. Luckily, I listened to it first. I gave my mother all her messages except for that one."

"Boy, were you lucky."

"Yeah, that reminds me," said Emma. "Danielle's message is still on the tape. If my mother hits the button again to hear her messages for herself, it'll come up. I need you to call here and just say anything, so it tapes over Danielle's message."

"I don't know what to say," Lindsey protested.

"My mother's a literary agent. She helps people get their books published. Pretend you wrote a book and you want her to sell it, but act weird so she won't want to call you back. Hurry up, you have to do it now while she's in the shower. Otherwise she might pick up the phone herself."

"Emma, I can't. I don't know what to—"

"Come on, just say anything. Thanks. 'Bye." Emma hung up with a quick click.

Oh, well, Emma was counting on her, and Mrs. Guthrie wouldn't know who it was. Lindsey thought for a few moments and then remembered a nature show Aunt Mariel had insisted on watching the other night on the educational channel. It gave her an idea. Taking a deep breath she redialed Emma's number. After two rings the tape clicked on. "You have reached Simone Guthrie. Please leave your name and a message when you hear the tone. Thank you."

"Hell*oooo,*" Lindsey spoke in a high, nasal voice. "This is Mrs. Noseblower from . . . um . . . the Department of Zoos. I've, ah . . . written a book on the wild anteater, a *mahvelous* subject of interest to nature lovers everywhere." Lindsey stifled the urge to burst out laughing. She could just picture Emma on the other end, listening and giggling. "I'm sure my new book will also be bought by ants all over the world and—"

"Ahem!"

Lindsey whirled around and found her father standing in the bedroom doorway. She slammed the phone down. "Hi, Dad."

"I thought Mariel sent you to your room," he said, folding his arms across his chest.

"She did. I, uh, had to make a phone call first," Lindsey spoke through the guilty lump in her throat.

"I guess prank phone calls are urgent," he said sarcastically. "They have to be made when the urge hits or they go flat." Lindsey wanted to smile at that, but since her father wasn't smiling she kept a serious face.

"I'll go to my room now, if you want," she volunteered.

"I think that might be a good idea. We'll talk about what happened this afternoon and about the use of the phone around here after supper."

"I could have supper in my room."

51

Her father looked at her and frowned. "No, since Mariel's here I want you to make an appearance at supper. You and I will talk afterward."

Lindsey hung her head and walked out the door past her father and across the hall into her room. She threw herself facedown onto her bed. For someone who didn't want to get into trouble, she thought, she'd managed to get in pretty deep.

Okay, Lindsey Munson, she said to herself, *stop being such a wimp. Emma's right. This is a war. If I want to stay here with Dad, then I'd better start acting up right now.*

Lindsey got up and walked to the doorway. "I'm not me, Lindsey," she whispered to herself as she opened the door. "I'm someone else. Someone terrible."

She started whistling a tune from the radio and clomped loudly down the stairs. She heard her father and Aunt Mariel talking in the kitchen. "Come on, Mariel," her father said, "this is harmless stuff. I was a lot like Lindsey when I was her—"

"When's supper?" Lindsey asked, boldly interrupting. "I'm starved." Ignoring the shocked looks on their faces, Lindsey picked up the lid of a pot on the stove and dipped her fingers into the mashed potatoes. "Kind of lumpy," she commented, licking her fingers clean.

"Lindsey, really!" gasped Aunt Mariel.

"I thought I told you to stay in your room until supper," her father said evenly.

"It's too boring in there," Lindsey said, opening the refrigerator and taking out a piece of plastic-wrapped chocolate layer cake.

"We're about to eat," Aunt Mariel reminded her.

"I'm not eating that slop," she answered, breaking

off a big piece of cake with her fingers and popping it into her mouth. She continued to stare at the cake, not looking at her father.

"Apologize to your aunt, young lady," her father ordered, standing in front of her.

"For what?" Lindsey mumbled with her mouth full of cake. "I didn't do anything. She's the one who made the slop."

She took a quick glimpse up at her father and was horrified to see that his face was beet red and his green eyes looked like they were about to pop out of his head. She'd never seen him this angry. She swallowed hard.

"I think you'd better go to your room right now," he muttered through clenched teeth.

Lindsey forced herself to be brave. "Okay, okay," she said as coolly as she could manage. "I'm going. I don't know what you're getting so hot about."

"Move! Now!" her father roared.

All Lindsey's false bravery disappeared as she bolted out of the kitchen and up the stairs. She leaned up against the Mets poster hung on the back of her door. Her heart was pounding. Hot tears spilled out of her eyes. She covered her face with her hands and let the tears run down her cheeks.

Emma made it sound so easy. Being horrible wasn't easy, though. It was hard and it felt awful.

She moved to her bed and sat on its edge, crying into the pillow she held on her lap. What must her father think of her? She didn't want him to hate her. She was doing all this just so she could stay with him.

Lindsey lay back on her bed. The dusky rays of twilight filtered through her blinds. It was almost dark, and Lindsey suddenly realized that she was very tired.

54

She shut her eyes and when she opened them again the room was almost pitch black. The red numbers of the digital clock told her it was nine-thirty. She sat up in bed and soon became aware of voices downstairs. She tiptoed to her bedroom door and opened it a crack. Her father and Aunt Mariel must have been talking near the stairs because their voices were very clear.

Her father spoke in an agitated voice. "As of this morning I'd decided that Lindsey was staying with me no matter what. But now I don't know. I've never seen this side of her before."

"She's growing up, Frank," said Aunt Mariel. "She's starting to feel rebellious."

There was a long silence. "I understand that," he said at last, "but this is so sudden. It's as if she's gone out of control almost overnight."

"Perhaps it just seems sudden to you," Aunt Mariel said in a gentle voice. "It's possible that it's been building up for a long time and you've been too busy to notice. It's not easy raising a child on your own."

A wave of panic swept over Lindsey. She wanted to run downstairs and cry out that her father was right. The change was sudden because it wasn't the real Lindsey at all. But she stood frozen at her bedroom door, listening.

There was more silence and then she heard her father sigh deeply. "I don't know, maybe she does need a regular family," he said, sounding beaten. "Maybe she *should* live with you. Let me think about it some more."

Seven

Lindsey woke up the next morning with a dull headache and a queasy feeling in the pit of her stomach. She sat up in bed and then lay back down. She was definitely too sick to go to school—too sick to get out of bed, even.

Her father rapped on her door at ten to eight. "Are you up?"

"I'm sick," she told him in her smallest voice.

He came in and stood by her bedside. He was dressed in his red pullover sweater, blue shirt and tie, and gray pants. His thinning brown hair was combed neatly, but still something about him looked all wrong to Lindsey. She realized it was his face. There were dark circles under his eyes, and he'd missed small patches of stubbly beard, as if he hadn't been concentrating when he shaved.

"You don't feel warm," he said, holding his hand on her forehead. "What hurts?"

"My stomach and my head," she whimpered pitifully.

He stood and studied her a moment, as if he was deciding whether or not she was faking. "Okay," he said at last, "go back to sleep."

She nodded and slid down under the covers. He looked like he was about to say something else, but then thought better of it. "See you tonight," he said, and left the room.

Tears welled in Lindsey's eyes. She wished he'd kissed her good-bye, or at least smiled at her. She didn't even know how to act with him anymore. Was she supposed to be bratty or go back to being herself? Would it make any difference if his mind was already made up? Was he forgetting about her already?

At about eight-thirty, Aunt Mariel came in with a tray of hot cereal, toast, and juice. "I hear you're not feeling too well today," she said pleasantly as she laid the tray down beside Lindsey. "Is it possible that you have a sickness known as a guilty conscience?"

Lindsey wanted to leap out of the bed and strangle her aunt. "I feel sick, that's all," she said, turning her head away.

Aunt Mariel's lips tightened into a disapproving line. "Okay," she said, and left the room.

Lindsey took a spoonful of the oatmeal, but she could hardly swallow it. Once again, tears ran down her cheeks.

She slept a great deal on Thursday. On Friday she still felt sick. Aunt Mariel refused to let her come downstairs and watch TV on the sofa, as her father always did when she was sick, so she spent most of the day looking through her back issues of *Sports Round-Up*. She pretended to be asleep every time Aunt Mariel came in with food or to check on her.

By Friday evening she realized what she had to do.

It was simple, really. She'd have to be the perfect child. There couldn't be any slipups. She would show Aunt Mariel and her father that she was doing perfectly well just as things were. She rolled over and settled in to sleep. Tomorrow morning the world would see a new Lindsey.

On Saturday morning Lindsey came down neatly dressed and ready for Mrs. Clark to pick her up for ballet. "Are you sure you're well enough?" asked Aunt Mariel at the kitchen table.

"I feel much better," said Lindsey politely. "Thank you very much for asking."

Her father, who was sitting across the table, lowered his paper and eyed her suspiciously. "Are you sure you're actually going to ballet class this time?" he asked.

"Yes, Dad," said Lindsey. "I'm sorry about the other day. It will never happen again."

Her father's eyes darted over to Aunt Mariel and then back to Lindsey. "I certainly hope not."

"I just wanted to remind you that you're supposed to pick us up today, Dad."

"No, I'm not."

"Don't you remember?" Lindsey asked in an exasperated tone. "Mrs. Clark called you the other day to—" Realizing that she sounded disrespectful, Lindsey cut herself short. "The three of us could take the bus home if you can't make it, Dad. It wouldn't be any problem, really."

Mr. Munson narrowed his eyes and stared at his daughter. "I remember now," he answered. "I'll be there."

"The bus is out of the question," added Aunt Mariel. "It's much too dangerous."

Who asked you, you child snatcher? Lindsey thought. "That's very true, Aunt Mariel," she said instead. "It was a foolish idea."

Lindsey excused herself and went outside to wait for Mrs. Clark. When she climbed into the Clarks' car, she was still on her best behavior, not wanting any bad reports to make their way back to her father. She knew parents talked to one another. Lindsey sat quietly in the backseat and answered in her new superpolite manner only when spoken to. "Yes, I'm feeling fine today, thank you very much," and "No, Emma, no bubble gum for me, thanks."

"I think that whatever was wrong with you these last few days affected your brain," Emma announced bluntly as they approached the mall.

"Yeah, it's like some alien space creature has taken over your mind," Charlie agreed. "It's turned you into a goody-goody zombie or something."

"Leave Lindsey alone," Mrs. Clark scolded as she turned the car into the mall parking lot. "I think she's setting a very good example by trying to mind her manners."

Charlie and Emma rolled their eyes and glanced at one another. Lindsey wanted to tell them what was going on, but she didn't dare risk it in front of Mrs. Clark.

Charlie's mother walked them down to the front of Miss Claudine's. "I'm going to stand here and make sure you go in and stay in," she told them.

"Mom, you don't have to do that," Charlie said. "I told you we wouldn't cut out anymore."

59

"All right, you did say that," Mrs. Clark agreed, leaning down to give her daughter a kiss on the cheek. "Have a good class."

"You won't regret trusting us, Mrs. Clark," Lindsey said.

Emma gave Lindsey a disgusted shove on the shoulder. "Get going, would you? What's the matter with you today?"

Once they were safely inside Miss Claudine's Lindsey told them what she was up to. She explained how Emma's plan had backfired. "So now he thinks he's raised me wrong, and it's all your fault, Emma. I have to be supergood from now on," she finished.

"Gosh, I'm sorry," said Emma sincerely. "I was positive it would work."

"Yeah, well it didn't," Lindsey told her.

The three girls looked around the front room for Miss Claudine. She wasn't there. They changed and headed for the studio. Standing in the middle of the class was a short, very old woman dressed in a long brocade dress and leaning on a cane. Her snowy white hair was pulled back severely into a bun.

She rapped her cane loudly on the floor for attention. "I am Madame Toumanova," she announced with a heavy Russian accent. "Miss Claudine has asked me to teach her class since she has now the flu as well as a bad ankle."

The students began murmuring their sympathies.

"Silence!" commanded Madame Toumanova with another loud rap of her cane. "I can see Miss Claudine has failed to instill this class with the discipline necessary for you to become great ballerinas. I once taught

60

Claudine, so it is up to me to correct this mistake in her class."

"Madame," Danielle said as she stepped forward from the line of girls near the barre, "I don't really belong in this class. I'm really in intermediate, but I always come to the beginner class to help Miss Claudine. I'd be happy to demonstrate for you." Danielle smiled proudly.

Madame Toumanova walked over very close to the girl. She studied her from head to foot and then leaned in until she was almost nose to nose with Danielle. "So you think I am so old and decrepit that I cannot demonstrate for myself," she growled.

"No, madame," Danielle stammered. "I just wanted to—"

"I can still demonstrate anything that needs demonstrating," the old woman bellowed. "I am not dead yet!"

"Yes, madame. I'm sorry, madame," Danielle muttered, bowing her head and backing away from Madame Toumanova.

A ripple of giggles spread through the class. "Silence!" the woman shouted, beating the floor with her cane. The class was instantly quiet. "Now we will begin with pliés in first position." Madame Toumanova turned on the rickety old record player, and the class began to bend their knees in unison.

"I hope Miss Claudine comes back soon," Charlie whispered to Emma, who stood in front of her at the barre.

"Yeah, I don't think I can take too much of Madame Apple Turnover," Emma agreed.

Lindsey, who was in front of Emma, wanted to laugh

at Emma's nickname for the teacher, but she stopped herself. She wasn't going to be getting into trouble today.

Madame Toumanova put them through their paces very slowly, correcting their posture, the placement of their feet, everything. Even Danielle didn't escape criticism. "You stick your behind out like a donkey," Madame Toumanova scolded her.

Once again the class giggled. Madame Toumanova beat her cane on the floor. "You girls are a disgrace!" she barked. "We will do nothing but barre work today. You are not fit to do anything more."

By the middle of class, Lindsey was bored with the barre work, and her mind started to wander as she went through the different steps. She imagined poor Miss Claudine as a young girl studying under this harsh old woman. It must have been terrible.

In her imagination she saw Aunt Mariel standing in Madame Toumanova's place. She pictured Aunt Mariel rapping the teacher's cane on the floor and criticizing her. "Lindsey, you set the table wrong. Lindsey, your clothes look terrible; iron that shirt. Lindsey, mind your manners. Lindsey, stand up straight."

A sharp jab on the shoulder roused Lindsey from her daydream. "Stand up straight!" shouted Madame Toumanova.

Lindsey straightened her posture, but Madame Toumanova wasn't satisfied. Again, she jabbed Lindsey's shoulder with a bony finger. "Get those shoulders down. You look like a no-neck thug."

Lindsey forced her shoulders down.

"No, no!" scolded the old woman. "Don't stick your

neck up and out like that. You make an absurd appearance."

Suddenly something inside of Lindsey snapped. It was as if she were seeing two faces in front of her, that of Madame Toumanova, and that of Aunt Mariel—and they were both ordering her around. Nothing she could do would ever satisfy either of them.

"Leave me alone!" Lindsey shouted. "You're not in charge of me."

"Enough!" Madame Toumanova boomed. "What is your name?"

"Lindsey Munson."

"Lindsey Munson, you are dismissed from this class. You are never to return. Miss Claudine will abide by my wishes. Now go!" Madame Toumanova pointed dramatically toward the door.

Lindsey started to walk. And that's when she saw a pair of green eyes staring unhappily at her from the entranceway. Her father had come by early—and he'd witnessed the entire scene.

Eight

"It doesn't feel right going to class without Lindsey," Charlie said as she and Emma walked through the mall toward Miss Claudine's the following Wednesday afternoon after school.

"I know," Emma agreed. "That Madame Somethingova is a real witch. She didn't have to kick Lindsey out. I can't stand her. Want to cut?"

"No. I told my mother I wouldn't."

"So?"

"So, I promised. A promise is a promise."

Emma shrugged. "Okay. I was really surprised when Lindsey shouted at old Somethingova. She doesn't usually do stuff like that."

"I think this whole Aunt Mariel thing is getting to her. If someone wanted to take me away from my parents, I'd go crazy, too."

"I guess," Emma said thoughtfully. "I miss my father a lot since the divorce. It really stinks."

Charlie looked at her friend, not quite knowing what to say. She suddenly felt very lucky to have both her parents. Death and divorce were both things she didn't want to think about too much. "You still have your mother," she reminded Emma, "and you see your father a lot."

"Yeah," said Emma. For a moment she looked wistful, as if her thoughts were very far away. Then she snapped back to her old brash self. "It's tough on Lindsey. She's only got one parent, and pretty soon she might not even have him. It's like being an orphan. We've got to think of some way to help her."

"Your last idea didn't turn out too well," Charlie reminded her. "And now poor Lindsey can't even come to ballet class. She's sure having a lot of bad luck these days."

The girls pulled open the door to Miss Claudine's. The other students were running around, chatting and fixing their hair as usual. There was still no sign of Miss Claudine—or of Madame Toumanova.

Danielle fluttered by and then turned back to look at Emma and Charlie. "The Three Musketeers are no more," she said with a smug little smile. "One down, two more to go."

"Shut up or I'll kick your little donkey behind," Emma snapped.

Danielle didn't like being reminded of Madame Toumanova's embarrassing remark. She spun around on her heel and continued on into the studio.

"Hey, look," Charlie said, poking Emma, who was busy glaring angrily in Danielle's direction. Emma turned and saw a tall woman with copper-colored, shoulder-length hair coming out of Miss Claudine's office. She wore a bright red leotard and tights over her curvy figure. "I've seen that woman before," Charlie said.

66

"You probably saw her in a makeup ad. She's got enough of it on," Emma cracked. "I mean, I like makeup and all, but enough is enough."

Charlie studied the woman, who was now going through the papers on Miss Claudine's big desk. She was indeed heavily made up, with her eyelids streaked in different shades of brown and gold. Her wide mouth shone a glossy, coppery red. "Look at that picture over her shoulder," Charlie told Emma.

Emma looked up at the familiar black-and-white photo of Marion Sweeney, Miss Claudine's famous Rockette student, and her eyes lit up. "Oh wow! You're right. It's her!"

"I wonder if she's still a Rockette," said Charlie.

"I always used to see the Rockettes at Radio City when we lived in Manhattan," said Emma. "I don't remember ever seeing her there, but it's hard to tell what they look like when they're all lined up and kicking their legs in the air."

Marion Sweeney looked up, as if she'd sensed their eyes on her. She smiled and pointed to the picture over her head. "Yeah, that was me when I was just starting out," she said in a low, raspy voice. "Now chop, chop, kids. Go get dressed."

"What happened to Madame Whatever-Her-Name-Was?" Charlie asked.

"She couldn't cope. Apparently you kids are a handful for an old lady. Now come on, hurry up, go," she said, shooing them toward the dressing room with her hands.

"She's bizarre," muttered Emma.

"Better than Madame Blah-blah-blah," Charlie commented.

67

"We'll find out."

By the time Emma and Charlie got to the studio, the other girls were already starting to line up at the barre. "Okay, so we start with pliés, I guess. Right?" said Marion Sweeney, walking to the center of the room.

"We begin with pliés in first, and go through the positions up to the demi-plié in fifth," Danielle volunteered. "If you need to know anything, ask me. I'm Miss Claudine's right hand. I actually belong in intermediate."

Marion Sweeney eyed Danielle coolly. "Okay, kid. I'll keep that in mind." She turned on the old record player. "Start pliéing your little hearts out," she told the class.

They'd finished the pliés and had begun doing arabesques at the barre when the music suddenly came to a screeching stop. All eyes turned to Marion Sweeney, who'd taken the record off. "Man, you guys look bored out of your skulls," she said. "Since I don't know where Claudine wants to go with this class, I'm going to try something different today. Sit down on the floor a sec."

Marion Sweeney pulled a chair into the middle of the room. "I'm going to fill you in on a few realities. First off, not all of you are going to get to be ballerinas. Some of you are going to lose interest and others of you are just never going to be good enough to hack it. I'm not saying that to be mean—it's just that not everyone was meant to be a dancer. That's just how it goes. And then, still, others of you aren't going to have the bodies for ballet. Either you're going to get too tall or too curvy, or both. That's what happened to me. I was five-ten and built by the time I was fifteen. I mean, could you really picture me in a line with all these dainty little ballet dancers? No way."

The class giggled nervously. It was true, Marion Sweeney didn't look like the delicate ballerinas they'd seen on TV and in pictures.

"There's still a lot you can do with your training, though," Marion Sweeney continued in her low, warm voice. "You can go into other kinds of dance. There's modern dance and there's chorus work—like in Broadway shows, or like what I do in the Rockettes."

Danielle made a disapproving "humph" sound at Marion Sweeney's last remark.

"You have a problem with that?" Marion Sweeney asked her pleasantly.

"It's nothing personal, but I don't think anyone here actually dreams of being a Rockette." She looked over at Charlie and Emma. "Well, some of us might, on second thought."

"Well, if it's not your thing, it's not," said Marion Sweeney, flipping her coppery hair over her shoulders. "But let me tell you, not just anyone gets on Broadway or into the Rockettes. Hundreds and hundreds of people try out every year, and just a handful are picked. So if you want to be any kind of dancer at all, this is the place to begin to work at it."

Charlie raised her hand. "Do you have to study ballet to be a Rockmania Dancer, like on TV?"

"I'll bet you anything that the ones who make it studied ballet and modern dance for years," Marion Sweeney answered. "I heard from a friend that the last time they auditioned Rockmania Dancers, the line wrapped around an entire block—and in the end they only took five dancers."

Charlie had never been able to picture herself as a ballet dancer, but somehow the thought of being on TV and dancing on the same stage as rock stars sounded good. Maybe she would take her lessons a little more seriously, she decided.

"Were you ever in a Broadway show?" Emma asked.

"I was in a couple before I hooked up with the Rockettes," Marion Sweeney replied. "They were fun, but I like the Rockettes 'cause it's steady. Broadway shows end, and you always have to be auditioning for new shows."

Emma rested her chin on her hands. She could see herself dashing up Broadway on her way to dance in a big show, maybe even being the star dancer and having everyone applaud; then going out afterward to a restaurant with all the actors and dancers from the show. It might be a fun thing to do for a few years before she began her career as a serious painter.

"Come on, get on your feet," Marion Sweeney told them, rising from her chair. "I'm going to show you a couple of Rockette routines."

"I don't think Miss Claudine would approve," said Danielle stiffly.

"Oh, sure she would," said Marion Sweeney with a wave of her hand. "Who do you think coached me when I first tried out?"

"I'd rather not participate, just the same," Danielle said, walking out of the studio with her nose in the air.

Marion Sweeney shrugged her shoulders and then motioned for the class to get up. She ran them through a few steps. "Step front, then back, little kick to your right." When they'd mastered that, she continued, "Now cross right, step left, and big kick front." When she demonstrated the big kick, her leg flew straight up over her head.

"Now here's the really tricky part," she said. "Line up side by side and grab the shoulder of the girl on either side of you. Run through the steps while holding on."

"Hey, watch it," a thin blond girl snapped at Charlie when Charlie accidentally kicked her in the shins.

"Sorry," Charlie muttered.

It took a number of tries before the girls got the hang of working together. Finally Marion Sweeney ran over to the record player and flipped through the small stack of old albums until she came to one she liked. " 'Great Show Tunes,' " she read the title. "This will do."

The lively music filled the room and made it easier for the girls to keep in step. "And step and step, keep those chins up and smile!" Marion Sweeney coached, doing the steps with them. "Now kick. Higher! Higher!"

Before they knew it, the class was moving together in a spirited chorus line. Charlie and Emma turned to one another and smiled as they kicked their legs high up in the air.

"All right!" Marion Sweeney cheered. "Looking good! Looking good! Let's see you really kick. Touch those chins with your knees!"

When the record ran out, Marion Sweeney applauded the class. "You guys are really hot! Good work." She looked at her watch. "Hey, class is over. You were great."

"Too bad Lindsey had to miss this class," Charlie said breathlessly to Emma.

"Come with me," Emma said suddenly, grabbing Charlie by the wrist and pulling her over toward Marion Sweeney. "Excuse me," Emma said to the tall

71

woman, "My name is Emma Guthrie, and this is Charlie Clark. We have a question about our friend Lindsey Munson."

"Sure, Claudine told me about you three," Marion Sweeney replied as they headed for the door. "Claudine says you guys always stick together. Where's your friend? Is she sick?"

"No," Charlie told her. "Madame Whatever kicked her out of class last week and told her not to come back. But it wasn't really her fault. She's had a lot of problems lately and she's been kind of in the dumps, so—"

"Oh, tell her not to listen to that old bat Toumanova," Marion Sweeney said with a gravelly laugh. "Claudine thinks she's some kind of genius, which is probably true, but she's also a pain in the butt. I'm sure your friend's a good kid. Tell her to come back next week."

"Thanks," said Charlie happily.

"Yeah, thanks a lot," Emma said as Marion Sweeney disappeared into Miss Claudine's office. "This is great. Old Lindsey's back in class."

"I just thought of something, though," said Charlie glumly as they walked into the dressing room.

"What?" Emma asked, wasting no time in wiggling out of her leotard.

"Lindsey won't be able to take class at all if she has to move to Boston with her aunt. We may never see her again."

Emma sat down on the bench and bit her lip thoughtfully. "I hadn't thought of that," she admitted. "I just wish that Aunt Mariel would disappear!"

"Me, too," said Charlie, plopping down beside her. "Me, too."

Nine

"I thought this would make you happy," said Charlie over the phone to Lindsey. "She said you should come back."

"That's good and all," Lindsey replied flatly. "But what's the sense of coming back if I'm just going to move to Boston?"

"Has anyone actually told you you're going?" Charlie asked.

"No, but my father is walking around, not saying much of anything to anyone. You saw him after ballet that afternoon. He didn't yell at me; he just looked real serious. Well, that's how he's been. And Aunt Mariel is so cheerful that it's sickening. I wish they would just come out and tell me what they've decided."

"Why don't you just ask them straight out?"

Lindsey hesitated a minute before she answered. She'd tried several times to get up the courage to talk to her father, but she hadn't been able to. Somehow it seemed to her that as long as nothing was said, there was a chance that the whole thing would go away. Once the words "You'd be better off living with Aunt Mariel" were spoken, then it would all become real. "I don't know," she said, "I just can't, that's all."

"You have to," Charlie urged her.

Lindsey knew Charlie was right. She decided to force herself to say something that evening.

Aunt Mariel made veal parmesan for dinner that night. At the table she chattered merrily about the summers she still spent in Newport, horseback riding and sailing. Mr. Munson and Lindsey both ate quietly, making only the briefest comments in response to Aunt Mariel.

Before she went to bed, Lindsey noticed her father's bedroom door was open. He was sitting on the edge of his bed, turning the pages of a large book. Lindsey decided that this was her chance to talk to him.

She walked over and knocked gently on the door. He looked up at her with tired eyes. "I was just looking through some old pictures," he said, nodding toward the photo album on his lap. Lindsey didn't recognize the book. Her mother had always kept their family pictures in blue albums starting with her marriage to Lindsey's father and continuing up until a few months before she died. After that there were no more albums. Her father threw any photos they had into a shoe box.

This album was orange with gold trim. The pages inside were yellowed, and so were the photos. "This was your mother's album from when she was little," her father explained.

Lindsey sat beside him and looked at the pictures. The early ones were in black and white. They showed a toddler and a girl in her early teens with their mother and father. The later pictures were in color. Most of them were of Lindsey's mother and her father, or just

of her mother alone. Some showed her with her mother and Aunt Mariel on the grounds of a fancy house with a sprawling green lawn. They were all taken during the summer.

"There's some difference, huh," Mr. Munson said, almost as if he were talking to himself.

"Difference in what?"

"The life your mom had with her father, and the one she could have had with her mother and her new stepfather."

"But she loved Gramps."

"I know, but he should have let her go where she could have had a better life. He should have insisted."

"Maybe she didn't want to go."

"She was just a child. That's the kind of decision adults have to make for children. If her father hadn't been so selfish, your mother could have had lots of opportunities her father couldn't provide."

"Like what?" Lindsey asked.

"Like going to a better college, meeting a different class of people. Having wonderful vacations instead of working every summer to make extra money." Mr. Munson turned and looked into his daughter's eyes. "You do look a lot like her."

Lindsey knew that this was the time to tell her father how she felt. She opened her mouth, but her tongue felt dry and no words could come out. She couldn't do it. She couldn't bear it if he told her he'd decided to send her away. "They said I could go back to ballet class," she finally said instead.

Her father nodded absently. "Good. No more mouthing off to the teacher, okay?"

"Sure," she said.

"You'd better get to bed," he said, kissing her on the cheek.

"Good night." She got a few steps into the hall and then turned back to him. "I love you, Dad."

"I know you do, Lindsey. Good night."

The next two days dragged for Lindsey. Nothing was said about Lindsey's going to Boston, but she overheard Aunt Mariel talking to her husband Miles, saying she'd be home by the middle of the next week, and that everything was all set.

"It doesn't sound good," said Emma that Saturday as they changed in the tiny dressing room of Miss Claudine's.

Lindsey just nodded in agreement. Things didn't sound good at all.

"Hurry up, kids!" Marion Sweeney stuck her head into the dressing room. She again wore her coppery hair loose over her shoulders. Today her leotard was bright green.

"That's her," Charlie whispered to Lindsey.

"I want Miss Claudine back," said Lindsey. "It's not right for her to let other people teach us. She's the one who's supposed to be in charge."

"She's sick," said Charlie.

"Well, I think it's about time she got better," grumbled Lindsey, walking out of the dressing room without waiting for Charlie and Emma.

Inside the studio, Marion Sweeney gathered the girls around her. "Claudine told me to say *'Bonjour, chéries,'* to all of you and to say she's very sorry for not being here. Between her ankle and the flu, she's feeling pretty low."

A rumble of sympathy for Miss Claudine swept through the class. "Hey, guess who else isn't here?" Emma whispered to Charlie and Lindsey as she looked around. "Danielle."

"Oh, I'll miss her so much. I don't know what to do," Charlie laughed.

"I cleared it with Claudine, and she said we could do some more precision chorus work today," Marion Sweeney told them with a grin. "She says it's good for your esprit de corps."

"What's that?" one of the girls asked.

"Teamwork," Marion Sweeney said. "Now line up, and let's go over what we learned last week." The girls stood next to each other and linked arms.

"But, wait, wait, I almost forgot," said Marion Sweeney, running toward a cardboard box near the door. "I brought these sashes to get you into the swing of things. Each of you take one and tie it around your waist."

The class broke from their line and gathered around Marion Sweeney as she handed each of them a wide satin ribbon. "Could I have a purple one?" Emma asked. "It's my favorite color."

"Sure thing," said Marion, pulling a purple ribbon from the box.

Emma took the ribbon and tied it around her waist. She studied herself in the mirror. She wasn't pleased. "Can I put another one around my wrist?" she asked.

"Hey, do what you like," Marion Sweeney answered with a smile. "Express yourself." The teacher turned to Lindsey and handed her a blue ribbon. "Here you go, kiddo," she said. "I'd say this goes well with those twinkly eyes."

Lindsey smiled at Marion Sweeney and tied the ribbon around her waist.

"Okay! Back in line, and let's see some high kicking!" Marion Sweeney told the class.

Lindsey wasn't sure what was happening. She meandered toward the end of the chorus line. "Hey, are you Lindsey?" Marion Sweeney asked. "Are you the kid that told Toumanova to take a hike?"

"I didn't mean to," Lindsey said shyly. "It was just that—"

"Hey, normally I'd say you should have minded your manners," Marion Sweeney said in a low voice, "but that Toumanova really pushes you." The dancer leaned toward Lindsey. "I got thrown out of her class, too. I told her to get off my case, just like you did. Sometimes you just have to speak up."

Lindsey smiled at Marion Sweeney. She felt good for the first time in a long while. "You just watch us go through the routine once, then join in," Marion told Lindsey.

The girls ran through their chorus. After a few times, Lindsey thought she had the hang of it and attached herself to the last girl on line. Marion Sweeney turned on the music and once again the class was swept along, kicking their legs in all directions.

"Kick straight up! Kick higher!" Marion Sweeney yelled. "And smile! Big smiles!"

Lindsey felt a great release from everything that had been weighing her down for the last few weeks. She kicked her legs into the air. "That's it, Lindsey!" Marion encouraged. "Watch Lindsey, class. That girl knows how to kick."

Lindsey felt slightly self-conscious as all eyes turned

to her, but she just kept flinging her legs up over her head. She never knew she could be so flexible.

"Let's see you all kick that high," Marion told the class. "Come on." Inspired, the class kicked its heels up higher than before. "Good!" yelled Marion. "Go for it! Nobody's going to know who you are if you don't let them know. Show them your stuff! That's my motto!"

Before any of the girls knew it, it was time for class to end. Marion Sweeney shut off the record and applauded the class. "Nice work!" she congratulated them. She walked over to Lindsey and put her arm around her. "Especially you, Lindsey. You're hot stuff. Come and see us in about seven or eight years if you're interested in being a Rockette. I'd say you've got what it takes. You have that inner spunk."

Lindsey smiled up at Marion Sweeney. "Thanks. It was fun," she said honestly. "Thanks for letting me come back."

"Hey, no problem," Marion Sweeney answered. "I think you're a great kid. Your parents should be real proud." The tall dancer jiggled Lindsey's shoulders affectionately and then headed out of the studio.

"You were great," said Charlie, joining Lindsey.

"The teacher sure liked you," Emma added. "She's neat."

"She did seem to like me a lot," said Lindsey, still feeling the warm glow of Marion Sweeney's praise. It had been so long since anyone had said—even suggested—that she was a great kid, she'd forgotten what it felt like. She'd even started thinking of herself as a problem.

"Want to come over my house?" Emma asked as they

81

headed toward the dressing room. "It will get you away from old Mariel for a while. Charlie's coming."

"Yeah, come on," Charlie said.

Lindsey thought a minute. "No, thanks," she said. "I'm going to go home. There's something important that I have to do."

Ten

Lindsey waved good-bye to Emma and Charlie as Mrs. Clark pulled out of her driveway. She pulled open the front door and walked into the living room. The house seemed quiet. "Anybody home?" she called. There was no answer.

She walked into the kitchen without taking off her jean jacket and looked out the back window. The door to the garage was open, and she saw her father inside.

Lindsey took a deep breath and headed out the back door to the garage. She waited in front of the open doorway for a minute before her father noticed her.

"Just cleaning up the garage. It's a mess," he said when he saw her standing there.

"Dad, I have to ask you a question," Lindsey said quickly, this time determined to get the words out before her mouth went dry. "Are you going to send me to live with Aunt Mariel?"

Her father stood very still. His face was serious and just a little pale. "Did Mariel tell you this?"

Lindsey nodded. "She said I should be thinking about it."

Mr. Munson's eyes narrowed and his face turned red with anger. "That woman!" he grumbled. "She wasn't supposed to say a word until I talked to you."

"It wouldn't have mattered," Lindsey said. "I heard you talking at night, anyway."

Mr. Munson leaned against the car and folded his arms. "I don't know what to tell you, Lindsey. I've been kicking this around in my mind day and night. It's a big decision." He unfolded his arms and rubbed his eyes and forehead wearily.

"Well, which way are you leaning?" Lindsey asked, trying to stay calm.

Her father studied her for a moment. "All right, we might as well just get this over with," he said. "Mariel can give you a good life. And you're getting older; maybe you need a woman around to guide you. What do you think?"

Lindsey felt as if she'd been hit in the chest with a very hard ball. Then suddenly she was very angry. "I think that you must not love me very much!" she shouted. "Otherwise you would never, ever think of giving me away."

Her father looked at her, stunned. "I'm not giving you away, baby. It's just that—"

"Yes, you are! You are!" cried Lindsey through the tears that now streamed down her cheeks. "And there's no reason to. Everyone around here has been talking about me like I'm some kind of problem. I'm not a problem! I'm a nice person."

"I know that, Lindsey—"

"You don't know it," she sobbed. "Aunt Mariel has you convinced that there's something wrong with the way I am, like I'm some kind of bad kid or something."

"Lindsey, I— " her father began.

"I just pretended to be a problem so Aunt Mariel wouldn't want me around."

Her father stepped forward and folded her in his arms.

"Daddy, don't let her take me. Please don't," she cried into his shirt.

He held her tightly and let her cry. "Nobody's taking you anywhere," he said, stroking her hair soothingly. "You're my baby. You'll always be my baby. I don't know what I was thinking."

After a few minutes Lindsey looked up and saw him brush a tear from his eye with the back of his hand. She dried her own eyes with the collar of her jean jacket. "Were you really going to send me away?" she asked seriously.

"Come on," he said, "let's take a walk." It was a sunny late-October day. The reds and oranges of the leaves seemed particularly vivid to Lindsey as she walked down the block with her father. "Mariel just about had me convinced that I was being selfish by not wanting you to go with her," he said as they walked. "She can offer you so much. And I thought maybe you did need a woman in your life."

"I think you're doing an okay job," said Lindsey.

Mr. Munson smiled at his daughter. "She just got me thinking about your mother. If she were still here, I figure she'd be doing a better job of it. She'd make sure you had pretty things to wear. She'd know what you needed."

"I have everything I need."

"Do you?" he asked. "You don't miss having a

woman to go shopping with and to talk about . . . I don't know, about girl things?"

"I don't know. I do miss talking to Mom. But talking to Aunt Mariel isn't anything like talking to her. You're more like Mom was than Aunt Mariel will ever be."

"But Mariel is a woman."

"I don't like Aunt Mariel very much," Lindsey said. "I'd hate to live with her. Besides, I'd miss you too much."

Her father looked at her and put his hand on her shoulder. "I'd miss you, too. Mariel is convincing, but she forgets about one thing."

"That we're doing fine without her?"

"Well, that, and she forgets about love—that I love you and you love me. I almost forgot that it was the most important thing myself. But I never forgot that I love you, Lindsey. You have to believe that the only reason I would ever even consider letting you go is because I thought it might be the most unselfish way to show my love."

Lindsey smiled up at her father. *I love you.* That was all she had really wanted to hear him say all this time. *I love you.* How good those words sounded! "I love you, too," she said. "And we'll always stay together?"

"For as long as you need me. I'm really sorry about this whole thing, Lindsey. Really sorry."

They walked down to Hardwood Road, where the traffic was busy. "Feel like a milk shake?" Mr. Munson asked, nodding toward the Purity Diner on the corner.

They went in and ordered two chocolate shakes to go. Then they walked back toward their house as they sucked on their straws. When they approached their

86

front yard they met Aunt Mariel walking up the driveway with a bag of groceries.

"I thought I'd make a nice chicken cordon bleu," she said to them.

Mr. Munson took the brown bag from her arms. "That sounds nice. But I think the three of us need to have a discussion first."

Aunt Mariel smiled at Lindsey. "Certainly," she said.

They went into the living room. Lindsey sat beside her father on the couch. They faced Aunt Mariel, who sat opposite them in the large blue chair. "Mariel, let me just come out and say it," her father began. "I've decided that Lindsey is going to stay here with me. We both appreciate your kind offer, but Lindsey and I are a family. I've given this more thought than you can imagine."

Aunt Mariel looked at Lindsey and Mr. Munson without any expression on her face. "Your mind is made up?" she asked at last.

"Yes, it is," Mr. Munson answered.

Again Aunt Mariel was silent for several minutes. When she finally spoke, it was in a low, angry voice. "Well, that is just about the most selfish thing I've ever heard in my life."

"She doesn't want to go, Mariel," Mr. Munson said calmly.

"How does this child know what she wants? It is totally irresponsible of you to let her influence your opinion, Frank. If you ask me—"

"I want to stay here, Aunt Mariel," Lindsey interrupted.

Aunt Mariel's eyes went wide. "It is just that very

lack of respect that I'm talking about. Lindsey is growing into an unruly, disrespectful girl."

"I am not!" Lindsey protested.

"She is not," Mr. Munson shouted at the same time. "Lindsey does well in school. She likes sports. She takes ballet. She has nice friends."

"Ballet! Nice friends!" Aunt Mariel hooted. "Those girls are a bad influ—"

Just then the doorbell rang. Lindsey ran to answer it. "What are you doing here?" Lindsey asked when she saw Emma and Charlie on her doorstep.

"Some greeting," said Emma. "We were just hanging around, so we figured we'd walk over and see how you were doing."

"I'd ask you to come in, but I don't think this is the greatest time," Lindsey told them, cracking open the glass storm door. As she spoke she turned and saw her father coming into the hall behind her.

"Ask your friends in, please," he said, pushing the storm door open. He ushered them into the living room, a hand on each of their shoulders. "Tell me these aren't sweet girls, Mariel. They're very nice friends for Lindsey. And I don't think they could spend their time more productively than studying ballet together."

"You have got to be joking," Aunt Mariel scoffed. "I'll bet you anything that none of them can show you one thing they've learned at that so-called ballet class in that . . . that shopping center."

"Sure we can," Emma spoke up. She ran over to the stereo and turned it on. She fiddled with dials until she came up with a station playing Broadway show tunes. "This will do, I guess," she said. "Come on, let's show your aunt what we learned today."

"Lindsey was the best in the class," Charlie said to Aunt Mariel as she put her arm up and formed a small chorus line with Emma and Lindsey. "Marion Sweeney said she could even be a Rockette some day."

The girls did the routine Marion Sweeney had shown them and soon they were kicking their legs up in the air happily. Once again Lindsey kicked up highest of all. She was so happy to know that she was going to stay right where she was.

Suddenly Aunt Mariel got up and snapped the music off. "Honestly, Frank, if this vulgar display doesn't convince you that Lindsey needs my guidance, then nothing will," she said.

"Then I guess nothing will," answered Mr. Munson with a twinkle in his eyes.

"There is obviously no point in my staying any longer," said Aunt Mariel stiffly. "I'll just pack and be on my way."

"That's up to you, Mariel," replied Mr. Munson.

Aunt Mariel squared her shoulders and drew her lips into a prim line. Then she turned and headed up the stairs.

When Aunt Mariel was out of sight, Emma and Charlie clapped their hands. *"Shhhh!"* Mr. Munson hushed them, his index finger held over his smiling lips. "Let's see that chorus line again."

Lindsey turned the radio back on and joined Emma and Charlie. They danced around the room, adding extra kicks and twirls to the steps, while Mr. Munson clapped along happily.

Emma and Charlie stayed for another hour. Charlie quickly turned and hugged Lindsey at the door before

she left. Emma punched her on the shoulder. "Glad you'll be stickin' around," she said.

"So am I." Lindsey smiled at them both.

Aunt Mariel stayed in her room until supper time. When she finally came down, she acted as if nothing had happened. "Miles has booked me a seat on the ten-o'clock plane tomorrow morning," she announced pleasantly when they were seated around the table, eating the plain chicken Mr. Munson had cooked under the broiler.

"No hard feelings?" Mr. Munson asked.

"Absolutely not," she said with a smile. She turned to Lindsey. "You are still my niece, and if you ever need me, you just call."

"I will, thanks," Lindsey answered. She felt the first glimmer of warmth toward her aunt, now that she was sure she was leaving. Nonetheless, she knew she'd feel better once Aunt Mariel was safely on her way to Boston.

By the time Lindsey walked toward Miss Claudine's with Emma and Charlie on the next Wednesday afternoon, Aunt Mariel seemed like a bad dream that was long over.

When they pushed open the door to the studio, there was the usual buzz of students getting ready for class. They were walking toward the dressing room when the door to Miss Claudine's office opened. There stood Miss Claudine. She stood without crutches, and she was dressed for class!

"*Chéries!*" she cried, arms stretched wide. "I have missed you all so very much!"

91

The class murmured their happy greetings. "Are you feeling better, Miss Claudine?" asked Danielle, coming out of the dressing room.

"*Magnifique!*" Miss Claudine said, a radiant smile lighting up her face. "Now we must hurry to work. I am anxious to see all you have learned in my absence."

"I guess the excitement's over," said Charlie as they headed into the dressing room. "I'm glad to see Miss Claudine again, though."

"Me, too," agreed Emma. "I kind of like having things back to normal."

Lindsey looked at her two friends and smiled brightly. "You can sure say that again!"

Don't miss NO WAY BALLET #3
Emma's Turn by Suzanne Weyn